Dance Just Like Me

17.

First published in 2010
by Wayland

Text copyright © Jillian Powell
Illustration copyright © Amanda Gulliver

Wayland
338 Euston Road
London NW1 3BH

Wayland Australia
Level 17/207 Kent Street
Sydney, NSW 2000

Series Editor: Louise John
Editor: Katie Powell
Cover design: Paul Cherrill
Design: D.R.ink
Consultant: Shirley Bickler

A CIP catalogue record for this book is available from the British Library.

ISBN 9780750260657

Printed in China

Wayland is a division of Hachette Children's Books,
an Hachette UK Company

www.hachette.co.uk

Dance Just Like Me

Written by Jillian Powell
Illustrated by Amanda Gulliver

WAYLAND

Clap your hands
just like me.

Stamp your feet
just like me.

Wave your arms
just like me.

Wiggle your fingers
just like me.

Shake your bottom
just like me.

Point your toes
just like me.

Kick your legs
just like me.

Nod your head
just like me.

Dance just like me!

Guiding a First Read of
Dance Just Like Me

It is important to talk through the book with the child before they read it alone. This prepares them for the way the story unfolds, and allows them to enjoy the pictures as you both talk naturally, using the language they will later encounter when reading. Read them the brief overview, and then follow the suggestions below:

1. Talking through the book
This girl is showing her friends how to dance to the music. She shows them all the different ways she can move her body to dance.

Let's read the title: **Dance Just Like Me**
Let's look at the pictures on page 4.
The girl says, "Clap your hands just like me."
Turn the page. Here she says,
"Stamp your feet just like me."
Now, turn to page 8.
What do you think she says here?

Continue through the book, guiding the discussion to fit the text as the child looks at the illustrations.

On page 18 the girl says, "Nod your head just like me." And on the last page, look! It's the same as the title – "Dance just like me!"

2. A first reading of the book

Ask the child to read the book independently, pointing carefully under each word (tracking), while thinking about the story. Praise attempts by the child to correct themselves, and prompt them to use their letter knowledge, the punctuation and check the meaning, for example:

Point underneath each word, not on top.
Well done. That's wonderful pointing!

You said, "March your feet". This makes sense, but what sound does 'march' start with?
Try it again and look carefully at the first word.
Yes, it starts with 's'. Could it be 'stamp'?

3. Follow-up activities

The high frequency words in this title are:
like   me

- Select a new high frequency word, and ask the child to find it throughout the book. Discuss the shape of the letters and the letter sounds.
- To memorise the word, ask the child to write it in the air, then write it repeatedly on a whiteboard or on paper, leaving a space between each attempt.

4. Encourage

- Reading the book again — with expression.
- Drawing a picture based on the story.
- Writing one or two sentences using the practised words.

START READING is a series of highly enjoyable books for beginner readers. **The books have been carefully graded to match the Book Bands widely used in schools.** This enables readers to be sure they choose books that match their own reading ability.

Look out for the Band colour on the book in our Start Reading logo.

The Bands are:

Pink Band 1A & 1B

Red Band 2

Yellow Band 3

Blue Band 4

Green Band 5

Orange Band 6

Turquoise Band 7

Purple Band 8

Gold Band 9

START READING books can be read independently or shared with an adult. They promote the enjoyment of reading through satisfying stories supported by fun illustrations.

Jillian Powell started writing stories when she was four years old. She has written many books for children, including stories about cats, dogs, scarecrows and ghosts. Jillian loves being outdoors, just like the children in Get Up and Go!

Amanda Gulliver always enjoyed art at school and went on to study Graphics and Illustration at College in Cornwall. Amanda now lives just a ten minute walk from the sea, where she can be found on the beach building sandcastles and collecting sea shells with her husband and two daughters.